In loving memory of Darren Greenfield, home at last

Text and illustrations copyright © Debi Gliori 2021

First published in Great Britain in 2021 and in the USA in 2022 by
Otter-Barry Books, Little Orchard, Burley Gate, Herefordshire, HR1 3QS
www.otterbarrybooks.com

ISBN 978-1-91307-463-0

Illustrated with charcoal and chalk

Set in Bembo

Printed in China

9 8 7 6 5 4 3 2 1

A Cat Called Waverley

Debi Gliori

Otter-Barry BOOKS

This is the story of a cat called Waverley.

Born in a park, Waverley learned how to hunt,
how to run from danger and how to make friends.

Lots of friends.

Every day, Waverley had breakfast
with a postman in Morningside,

lunch with old Mrs McKinnon
and her kitties in Corstorphine,

afternoon tea with the
soldiers at the Castle,

but best of all, supper, a hug and a warm bed for the night with his best friend, Donald.

This happy life went on for many years,
until one day Donald had to go far, far away.
So far away that Waverley couldn't come too.

Waverley tried to stow away in
Donald's kit bag, but that didn't work.

Waverley tried to stop Donald leaving,
but that didn't work either.

"Cat," said Donald. "You have to stay here.
My flatmates will look after you while I'm away."
But Waverley didn't understand what Donald
was saying. Waverley wanted Donald to stay.

He told Donald this,
but Donald didn't understand a word Waverley said.

Waverley followed Donald
until he could follow no
further, for even a cat
can't keep up with a train.

Poor Waverley.
What would he do
without his best friend?

One by one, his other friends
disappeared. A new postman
came to Morningside, and he
didn't like cats.

Old Mrs McKinnon
moved away and all
her kitties vanished.

One day at the Castle, there was
a huge BANG from the one o'clock gun
and Waverley never went back.

But worst of all, Donald's house
was knocked down and, just like that,
Waverley was homeless.

Edinburgh is full of places for a cat to live,
and there's no shortage of people who love cats.
However, Waverley didn't want to live anywhere
without Donald. Home was where Donald was,
wherever that might be.

So Waverley went to the station
and waited…

and waited…

and waited.

Soon, people began to notice
the lonely little cat
on Platform Two
at Waverley Station.

They called him Waverley because
they thought that was his home.
But Waverley knew home was
where Donald was, wherever
that might be.

People took photographs and
brought food for him. But even
though he was desperately lonely,
Waverley wouldn't let anyone
pick him up.

Nobody, that is, except Donald.

The station manager allowed Waverley
to sleep in his warm office overnight.

The cleaners shared their breakfast with him.

And best of all, once a week, a kindly train driver let Waverley help her drive the train. Together they travelled up to the Highlands and back.

Waverley peered out of the window,
wondering where Donald had gone.
Was he in that forest? On top of that mountain?

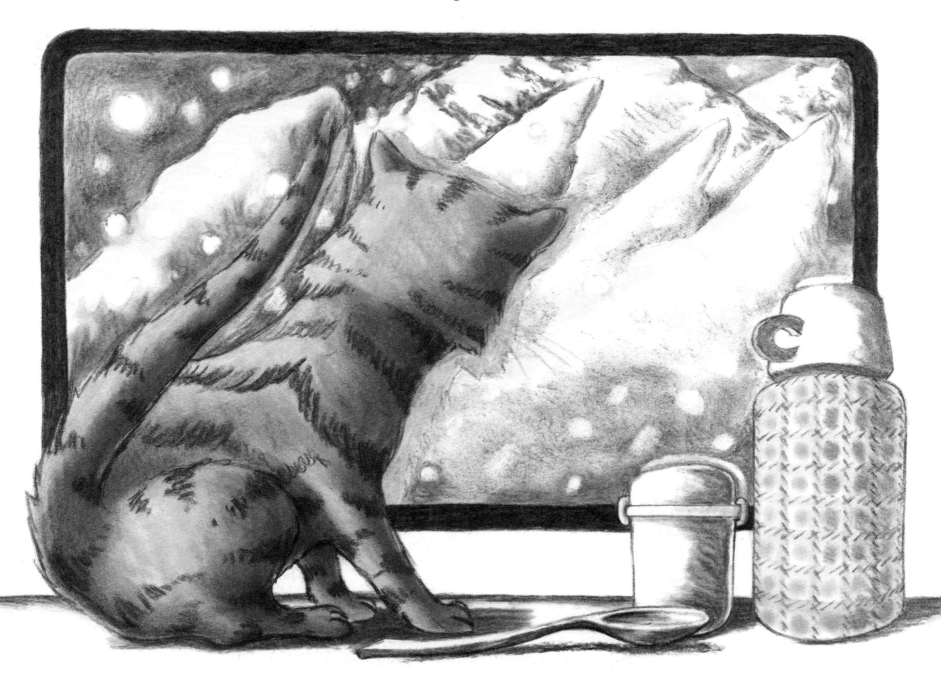

Waverley missed his best friend more and more

with each passing season.

This went on for many years until, one day,
on his way to Platform Two,
Waverley heard a familiar voice.
"Spare change," the voice said.
"Spare a few pence for the homeless."

There, sitting at the top of the station steps,
was Donald!

Waverley ran,
weaving through feet,
dodging suitcases until, at last,
he was in front of his friend.

"MIAOW!" he yelled and he jumped
onto Donald's lap, purring and turning
in circles and winding his tail round
and round like a furry propellor.

People stopped and stared.
Nobody had ever seen Waverley
do that before.

"Look," they said, "that must be the
man who belongs to Waverley."

"MIAOWWWWW," said Waverley, "I'm so glad you're home."

But there was something wrong with Donald. His face was all wet and Waverley could hardly understand a word his friend was saying.

But it didn't matter. It didn't matter one single bit. As he curled up in Donald's lap, Waverley knew he was home at last.

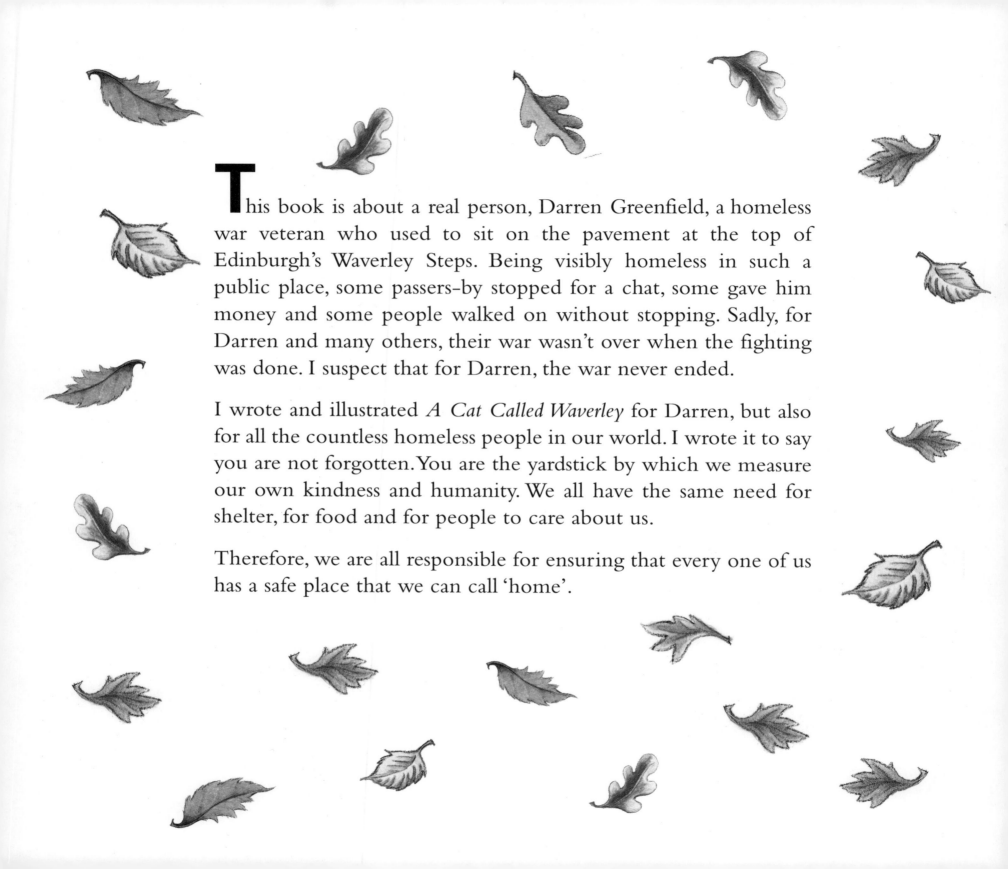

This book is about a real person, Darren Greenfield, a homeless war veteran who used to sit on the pavement at the top of Edinburgh's Waverley Steps. Being visibly homeless in such a public place, some passers-by stopped for a chat, some gave him money and some people walked on without stopping. Sadly, for Darren and many others, their war wasn't over when the fighting was done. I suspect that for Darren, the war never ended.

I wrote and illustrated *A Cat Called Waverley* for Darren, but also for all the countless homeless people in our world. I wrote it to say you are not forgotten. You are the yardstick by which we measure our own kindness and humanity. We all have the same need for shelter, for food and for people to care about us.

Therefore, we are all responsible for ensuring that every one of us has a safe place that we can call 'home'.